This Walker book belongs to:

_ _ _ _ _ _ _ _ _ _ _ _ _ _ _ _ _

_ _ _ _ _ _ _ _ _ _ _ _ _ _ _ _ _

_ _ _ _ _ _ _ _ _ _ _ _ _ _ _ _ _

FOR LITTLE B.I.T. - J.D.
FOR MY JOY, TED. - Y.I.

First published 2019 by Walker Books Ltd, 87 Vauxhall Walk, London SE11 5HJ

This edition published 2020

2 4 6 8 10 9 7 5 3 1

Text © 2019 Yasmeen Ismail   Illustrations © 2019 Jenni Desmond

The right of Yasmeen Ismail and Jenni Desmond to be identified as author and illustrator respectively of this work has been asserted by them in accordance with the Copyright, Designs and Patents Act 1988

This book has been set in Agenda and JenniDesmond   Printed in China

British Library Cataloguing in Publication Data: a catalogue record for this book is available from the British Library

ISBN 978-1-4063-9096-4

www.walker.co.uk

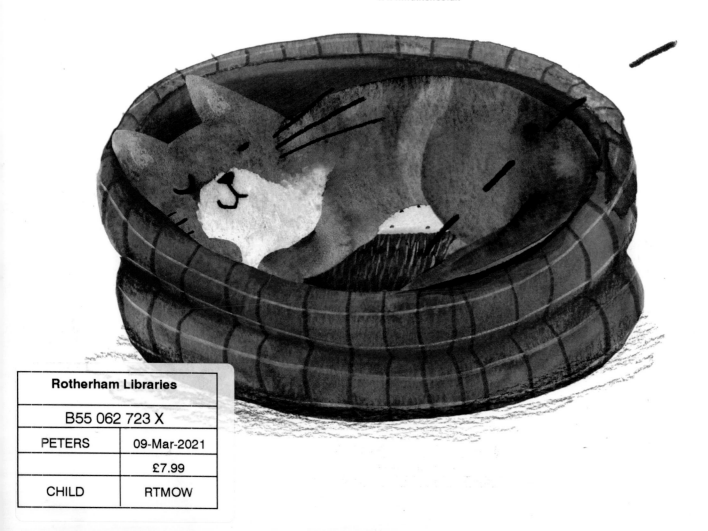

JOY

Written by
YASMEEN ISMAIL

Illustrated by
JENNI DESMOND

WALKER BOOKS
AND SUBSIDIARIES
LONDON · BOSTON · SYDNEY · AUCKLAND

Oh boy! Oh boy!
My favourite toy.
I feel joy!

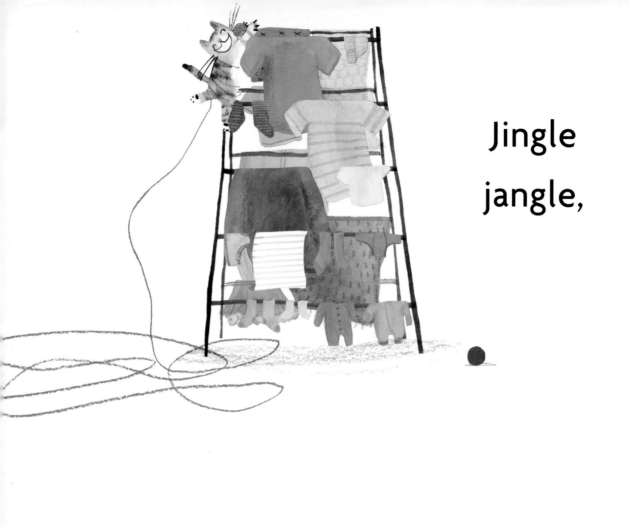

Jingle
jangle,

wriggle
wrangle,

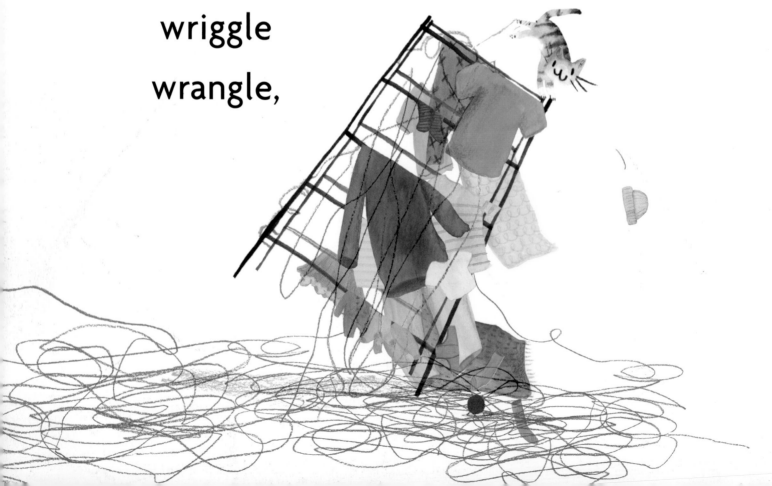

in

a

tangle.

BOUNCE BOUNCE BOING BOING

Shake,
rattle
and

ROLL,

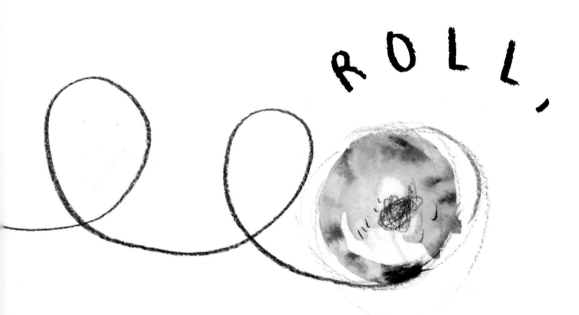

this happy soul!

Tickle, tickle,
in a pickle.

Run, run, fun, fun.

ZOOM-ZOOM   ZIM-ZAM

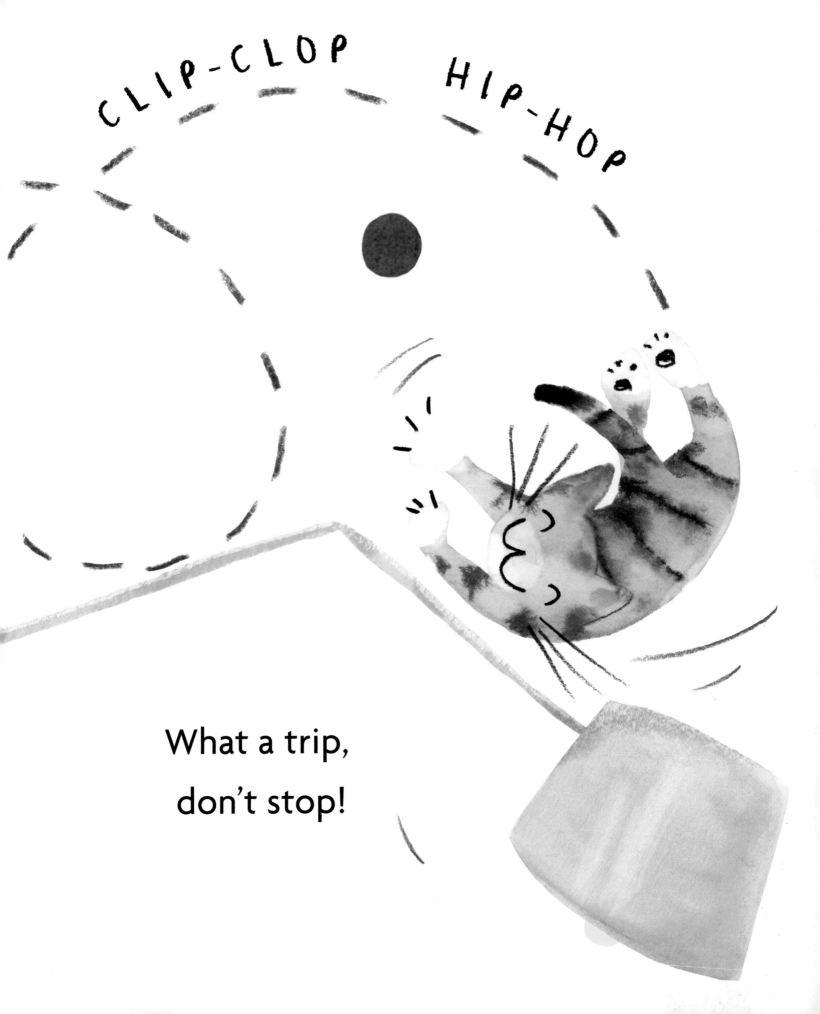

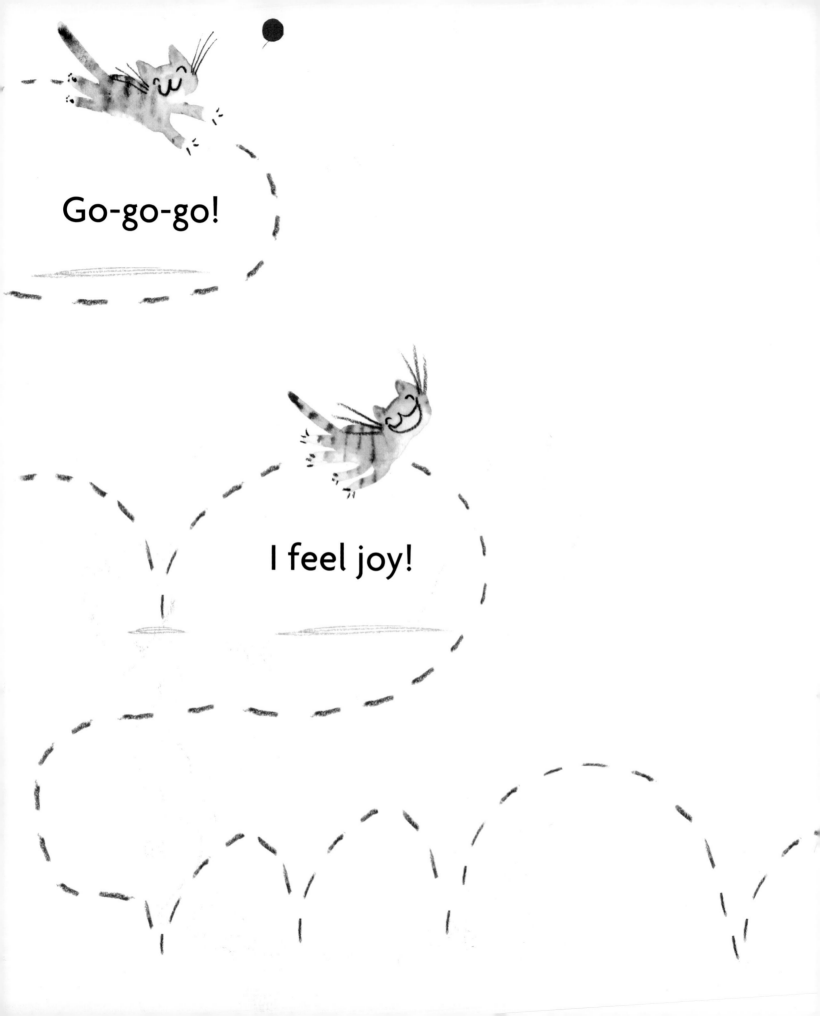

Go-go-go!

I feel joy!

UH-OH.

BING
BONG

DING
DONG

CRASH
BANG
WALLOP

BONK-
A-
DONK

DONK   Ow.

Oh...
This is bad.
I feel sad.

Where's my mum?
Where's my dad?

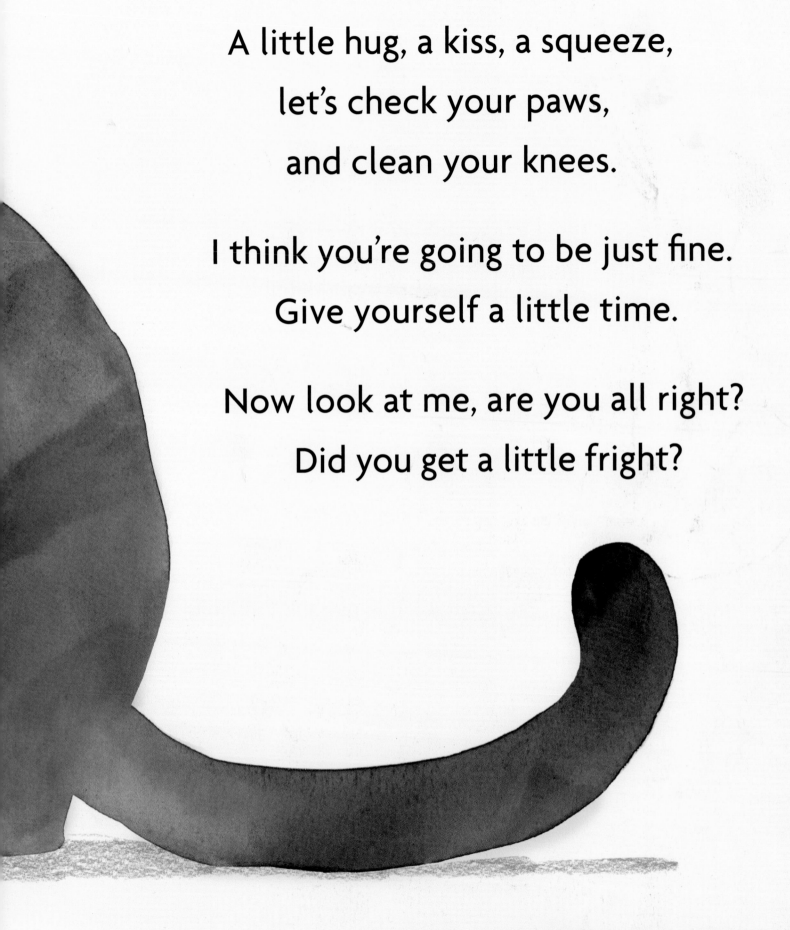

A little hug, a kiss, a squeeze,
let's check your paws,
and clean your knees.

I think you're going to be just fine.
Give yourself a little time.

Now look at me, are you all right?
Did you get a little fright?

I'm always here if you fall.
All you have to do is call.

There's nowhere that
I'd rather be,
than holding you
so close to me.

Oh boy!

Oh boy!

My favourite toy.

I feel joy!

Also by Yasmeen Ismail:

978-1-4063-8006-4

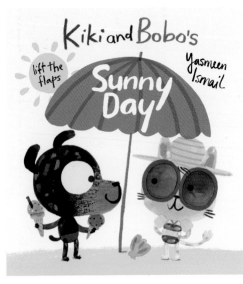

978-1-4063-7887-0

978-1-4063-7584-8

Also by Jenni Desmond:

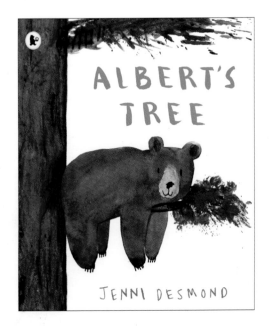

978-1-4063-6249-7

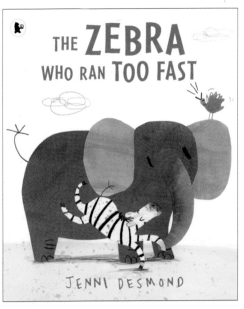

978-1-4063-6074-5

978-1-4063-7937-2